A Sea Change

Veronica Henry

An Orion paperback

First published in Great Britain in 2013
by Orion Books Ltd,
Orion House, 5 Upper St Martin's Lane,
London WC2H 9EA

An Hachette UK company

1 3 5 7 9 10 8 6 4 2

A CIP catalogue record for this book
is available from the British Library.

ISBN 978 1 4091 0401 8

Typeset at The Spartan Press Ltd,
Lymington, Hants

Printed and bound in Great Britain by Clays Ltd,
St Ives plc

The Orion Publishing Group's policy is to use papers that
are natural, renewable and recyclable products and made
from wood grown in sustainable forests. The logging and
manufacturing processes are expected to conform to the
environmental regulations of the country of origin.

www.orionbooks.co.uk

To my readers, old and new.
I hope you enjoy your trip to Everdene.

Chapter One

The M5 motorway on a Friday afternoon in August was enough to drive you mad. It took Craig forty minutes just to get out of the city. Then the traffic would be nose to tail all the way from Birmingham to Taunton. Stop–start. Stop–start. A slow crawl that had him drumming his fingers on the steering wheel.

Craig looked longingly at the hard shoulder. It was so tempting. If he got stopped, he could just flash his badge. He'd probably get away with it, except he wasn't that sort of copper. He didn't abuse his position. He had mates who had no problem with doing that kind of thing – breaking the rules – but Craig liked to stick to the letter of the law. He always played it straight, even if it wasn't always the easy option.

He could feel his T-shirt sticking to the back of his seat. He wasn't going to be a pretty sight by the time he got to the beach at Everdene, nor a pretty smell. The air-con didn't seem to make any difference, and opening the windows didn't help. He took a swig from the bottle of water he'd stuffed in the cup holder. It was warm, but it took the edge off the dryness in his throat. He wiped his brow with the back of his arm and looked at the sweat. Gross.

After Taunton, the traffic cleared and he put his foot down, keeping at a steady seventy miles an hour until he turned off the motorway. The car headed over Exmoor – its high, bleak landscape parched and brown from the summer sun. Away from the traffic Craig started to relax. He had a whole week off. A whole week to do what he liked. All he had with him was a few clothes, a wetsuit and his surfboard. And the key to the beach hut.

There were eight of them from the police station who'd clubbed together to rent the hut. Young people who were all into beach life and loved surfing, rock climbing, walking and kayaking. It was cheaper than going on holiday. It took just over three hours to get there, if you put your foot down, so between them they made the most of it.

Craig was the only one going down this weekend. All the others had different plans. After all the stress he'd had lately, he was looking forward to the peace and quiet. He couldn't wait to get there.

As he drove past the last supermarket before Everdene, he decided to pull over and pick up some food so he wouldn't have to venture out for a day or so. He bought a hot chicken and some rolls, a bag of salad, fruit, biscuits, some beers and bottled water. By six o'clock he would be sitting on the step, sipping a beer and looking at the sea.

As he left the car park he turned up the radio, grinned from ear to ear and gave a whoop.

Let the weekend begin.

Chapter Two

Jenna ran a damp cloth over the counter of her ice-cream kiosk for the tenth time that afternoon. She liked to keep it spotless. Behind her the radio was blaring, and above her the sun was shining in the sky. She adjusted the cones waiting to be filled, smoothed out the surfaces of the tubs and washed her scoops again. She looked down at the cabinet, pleased with the way it looked.

Inside there was a rainbow of ice creams to choose from. There were the usual, of course – chocolate and strawberry and vanilla. Then there were the more exotic flavours. Maple and walnut, rhubarb and ginger, Mississippi mud pie, peanut-butter cluster. The one that most kids seemed to hanker after was bubblegum, bright blue and sickly sweet. Dream Ices certainly didn't leave you short of choice.

The kiosk was situated at the top of the row of shops that led down to the harbour. Tawcombe had once been a thriving holiday resort, bursting at the seams with tourists. Now, in the recession, it was feeling the pinch. The hotels were closing down one after the other, as were the restaurants. Eventually the empty places got boarded up, then covered in graffiti, which didn't make the place very inviting.

The fishing boats still came in and out of the harbour, but there was a run-down air to the seafront, which had once bustled with life. Now it was deserted most of the day, until evening when gangs of bored youths collected there with cans of lager. The coastline was spectacular with its craggy rocks and crashing waves, but the town itself had become grey. A handful of attractions remained – a merry-go-round circled on the front, its horses in need of repainting. The arcade beeped and flashed with fruit machines.

And Dream Ices sold twenty-nine varieties of ice cream, which you could have in a waffle cone, or in a cone coated in sprinkles, or in a cone dipped in chocolate. You could also have chocolate, raspberry or butterscotch sauce on top. Then if you still wanted more, there were chocolate flakes and fingers of fudge and a squirt of whipped cream to finish.

Twenty-nine flavours had always annoyed Jenna. She would have made it thirty, but one of the tubs was filled with water for washing

11

the scoops. Three rows – two of ten and one of nine – of brightly coloured, mouth-watering ice cream. She had noticed over the past week that some of the tubs were nearly empty and hadn't been replaced. Usually they were filled up before you could see the white plastic at the bottom. They'd almost run out of rum and raisin, and mint chocolate chip, and Devon clotted-cream fudge. There wasn't any in the freezer, which was strange. When she mentioned it to her boss, Terry, he just nodded and said he'd get onto it.

Dream Ices had done OK. Even though times were hard, it seemed like people still had money for an ice. There were just enough day trippers to keep the place ticking over. Sometimes Jenna scooped away all afternoon. All the same, she should have sensed trouble coming. For some reason, she hadn't.

So when the owner of Dream Ices, Terry, came up to her on Friday afternoon, Jenna hadn't expected to be sacked.

'I've got some bad news, love,' he said. 'I was hoping this wasn't going to happen but times are hard. I'm going to have to let you go.'

Her eyes widened in shock. 'You're not closing down, surely?'

'No. Not yet.' He looked gloomy, as if this

might happen. 'But I can't afford to keep you on. I'll have to run the place myself.'

She wasn't sure how he was going to manage that. Terry spent most of his time in the pub or at the bookies. Maybe that explained why he was in difficulty.

'Things will pick up,' she said hopefully. 'We've been busy today. And the forecast for the weekend is great. Nearly thirty degrees, they reckon.'

Terry was always moaning that the glory days were over. He was always telling her about the life he used to have, when the town was in its heyday and his pockets were stuffed with cash.

He shook his head. 'Even if we doubled the takings in the next month, I can't afford you. I'm sorry.'

'Surely we've done all right this summer?' she asked. 'I've been rushed off my feet some days.'

He shook his head. 'Not like the old days. I could clear five hundred quid cash, no problem, on a bank holiday. I struggle to get that in a week now. And the rent's gone up. And the wholesalers have put their prices up.'

Jenna didn't know what to say. Terry looked out to sea and cleared his throat. 'I can't give you your wages, either.'

Jenna's heart skipped a beat. He owed her over two weeks' money.

'You're kidding me.'

'I haven't got it. I had to pay the supplier. There was nothing left.'

There had been enough for him to have a few pints at lunchtime. She could smell the beer on his breath.

'I'll bring it round when I get it,' he promised her. 'If we have a good weekend . . .'

She'd never see it. She knew that.

'You could have told me before,' Jenna told him. 'You must have known you couldn't pay me, but you let me carry on working.'

'No,' he said. 'I promise you. I was hoping for something to happen. I was hoping . . .'

'For a win on the horses?'

Terry gave something between a shrug and a nod. Jenna felt hot with fury.

'Gambling is a game for mugs. Surely you know that by now, Terry? If it was that easy, everyone would be doing it.'

Terry just walked away and stood by the harbour railings. He lit a cigarette.

Jenna couldn't believe what Terry had done. She had been so loyal to him. She'd kept the place afloat all summer, smiling and laughing with the customers. She talked them into having two scoops when they only wanted one. She persuaded women who were watching their figure that just one wouldn't hurt. And the locals came here to buy ice cream from her too. She'd become a bit of a local landmark over the summer. It was her banter rather than the ice cream that they came for. And her singing.

She'd started off singing along to songs on the radio, using a cone as a microphone. Then she started singing whatever she felt like, her own favourites that she could belt out behind the counter. It kept her sane even if she did look mad, but people seemed to enjoy it. Her mood was catching.

She was known as the Ice Cream Girl. She didn't mind being called that at all. It was a happy name. People had started making requests. They were always telling her she should go on *The X Factor*, or get an agent, or join a band. But Jenna knew there was a big difference between mucking about and doing it for real. She wasn't convinced she had any real talent. She just wanted people to have a good time.

She wasn't going to be the Ice Cream Girl any more, though. In the past two minutes she had been turned back into a nobody. That would teach her to have trusted Terry, and to have done her best for him. She had genuinely thought he would look after her and see her right, but no. As soon as things got tough he had dumped her. He was just like everybody else. Out for himself and what he could get.

She felt tears pricking the back of her eyelids, but she refused to cry. Terry Rowe wasn't going to see the effect he'd had on her.

She took off her apron and folded it up carefully. Then she picked up the strawberry sauce and squirted it all over every tub of ice cream in the cabinet. She followed it with the chocolate. Then she sprinkled a shaker full of hundreds and thousands over the lot.

She felt sick with anger. She remembered the number of times Terry had rung her, begging her to do a shift because he'd had a skinful. The days she'd stayed late because he couldn't drag himself out of the pub. He had repaid her loyalty by sacking her the minute things got tough.

He came back when he had finished his cigarette. She could smell the tobacco on him and it turned her stomach.

'What have you done?' he asked, outraged.

She shrugged.

'You can pay me back for all of that! There's a couple of hundred quid's worth there.'

'Take it out of my wages,' she told him.

It hadn't been a dream job. No one dreamed about selling ice cream the way they did being an actress or a supermodel or a singer. She'd enjoyed it, though. Ice cream brought a few moments of pleasure. She loved watching people's faces as they looked at what was on offer, dazzled by the choice. She loved their smiles as they took their loaded cones. There were worse jobs.

She walked away from the kiosk without looking back or bothering to say goodbye.

By the time Jenna got to the end of the quay, her anger had turned to fear. She felt anxious. So anxious that it felt like her insides were being eaten. It was turning out to be a bad summer. Three weeks ago, someone had broken into the house where she had a room. They'd smashed in all the doors and taken everything they could. Jenna didn't have much in the way of valuables. But she had had three weeks' worth of wages tucked into the back of a drawer, waiting to pay the rent.

Her landlord hadn't been at all understanding. He reckoned it wasn't his fault the house had been burgled, even though everyone said the locks hadn't been strong enough. He'd agreed to wait for the rent until Jenna got her next lot of wages, which should have been today.

How was she going to pay now? Her landlord was going to kick up, she knew he was. He wouldn't be interested in reasons or excuses. She'd promised him the rent she owed in cash by the end of the week, which was today. Friday. Otherwise he was going to boot her out. She knew he would. He knew people who would come and pack up her stuff and throw it out of her room, then drag her out afterwards. She'd seen it happen before.

It didn't matter where she stood legally. People like her landlord didn't take any notice of the law. They knew the system wouldn't look after her. She was a nothing, a nobody, and no one cared.

Jenna trudged into the centre of Tawcombe, past the chip shop and the arcade and back to her house. She'd never call it 'home'. Home was somewhere you were glad to come back to. Somewhere you felt you belonged. She was yet to feel that about anywhere.

Chapter Three

The last five miles of Craig's journey were along a winding road lined with hedges. On either side the fields were full of sheep and cows. At last he reached the roundabout that led down the hill to Everdene. After another half a mile and then, around the next corner, was the sight that lifted his heart every time he saw it.

The sea. Endless and blue, yet never quite the same colour. That first glimpse was always a thrill. He could see the pinky brown of the beach, too, which was more than a mile of soft, soft sand. Then when he got closer, he spied the candy colours of the beach huts lined up in a row. The one that he shared with his copper mates was the seventh one along. Pale blue and white and in need of a lick of paint, but they never complained. Who cared about the state of the paintwork when there was fun to be had?

He left his car in the public car park, took his overnight bag and his shopping from the boot and headed off down the slipway next to a small arcade of shops. They were all just closing for the night but he had time to buy himself a bag of chips from the café. He sat outside and ate them, one by one. Craig usually ate healthily, but he always treated himself every time he came down here. He'd soon burn off the calories.

He kicked off his shoes and made the last part of his journey barefoot. The heat of the day was still in the sand, although as he sank deeper it was cool beneath the surface. It was hard going with everything he had to carry, but at last he reached the seventh beach hut along, with its faded blue door. He pulled out the key and slid it into the padlock, unlocked it and stepped inside.

It always smelled the same, of damp and wood and salt. He breathed in and his stomach did a flip. It was like coming home. This was the place in the world where he felt most happy. It was basic. Some of the huts on the beach had been done up like show-homes, but this one had hardly been touched since it was put up over thirty years ago. It had four wooden bunks, a kitchen area with a couple of cup-boards, a tiny sink and a Calor gas stove. There was also a makeshift shower and a toilet. It was furnished with a giant old settee that sagged in the middle and a rickety table with four wobbly chairs.

The blokes who shared it made no effort to decorate the hut, but sometimes the girls tried to add a feminine touch. One had bought a set of matching spotted mugs, tired of the chipped and stained ones. Another had put up some surfing pictures, and another had strung up some fairy lights. They had an ancient ghetto blaster on which they played old cassettes. They had a competition to see who could dig out the most cheesy tape. Most nights the hut rocked to the sounds of Herb Alpert, Barry Manilow and Boney M.

Tonight, though, it was going to be peaceful. Craig preferred quiet when he was on his own. He needed to be alone with his thoughts, because he knew he was going to have to make a tough decision this weekend. As he looked out across the shore, he felt the worries and tension of the past few weeks gradually start to ease.

It was all very well knowing you were innocent, but that didn't always count for much, especially when it was your word against someone else's. And when the video evidence against you looked bad, you didn't have much of a chance. Craig knew he would never treat a police suspect with unnecessary violence. But

21

he'd been set up by a gang of blokes with a grudge against him. He'd been responsible for arresting one of their mates who'd been sent down for a long stretch. As a result, they'd stitched him up and had him accused of police brutality. He'd been suspended while there was an investigation. Craig had spent the entire three months leading up to his case convinced he was going to lose his job – or, maybe, even worse.

In the end, justice had been done and he had been found innocent, but the stress had taken its toll. He lived in fear of it happening again and now faced every day with dread. He was fine with his close friends, but felt awkward with other workmates he came into contact with. He could tell they were wary, wondering if he had been guilty. After all, there was no smoke without fire.

The whole episode had made him question what he was doing with his life. He'd been longing to escape back to Everdene, so he could clear his head. Now that he was here, he felt more hopeful. As he sank into a deckchair outside the beach hut and looked at the view with a bottle of beer in his hand, the future didn't seem quite so bleak.

*

Jenna finally arrived at the terraced house where she lived. She had a bedsit on the third floor. She shared a bathroom and kitchen with six other people. Six other people who didn't know how to use a dishcloth or bleach, or even flush the toilet, sometimes. She ended up cleaning up herself, even though they were supposed to take turns. It was either that, or live in squalor.

She'd tried to make her room as nice as she could, but it was difficult. The carpet was green with mould in the corners. The wallpaper was ancient and coming off the wall in clumps. The windows let the cold in through the cracks in winter and turned the place into a sauna in summer. She couldn't afford proper curtains, so she'd hung a pair of old sheets from the rail. On the walls, she'd stuck photos of her heroines: Marilyn Monroe and Dita von Teese – both glamorous pin-up girls not afraid to show off their curves. She tried to copy their image, but it was hard to look the part when you barely had enough money to keep body and soul together. Still, she always tried to wear a dress, and lipstick, and put her hair up, and this look usually helped to lift her spirits. If things were going badly, and you slobbed about in jeans and no make-up, you were bound to feel bad about yourself.

No amount of dressing up took away her fear, though. She sat in the middle of her bed. It would only be a matter of time before the landlord came knocking. She didn't have the money for her rent. Her stomach churned with dread. Where would she go if he kicked her out? She didn't think she could get any lower. She'd left her mum's house a year ago when their rows had got out of control. She'd thought she could stand on her own two feet. It was much harder than she thought.

Jenna thought about phoning her mates and meeting them at the pub, then she remembered she wouldn't be able to afford a drink. She was penniless. Someone would buy her one, of course they would, but she didn't want to feel like a scrounger. She flopped back down onto the mattress. The room smelled stale. The air was almost too hot to breathe. Everyone was saying what a fantastic weekend it was going to be, with soaring temperatures and fun in the sun.

There wasn't going to be any fun on the third floor of 21a Boscombe Terrace.

*

It was after his second beer that Craig began to miss Michelle.

He knew it would happen. The first drink relaxed you. By the second, your defences were down and emotions started to kick in. It would take another two or three beers to blot out the feelings altogether, but Craig didn't want to get drunk. He was going to have to put up with how he felt.

They'd gone out for five years, Craig and Michelle. It had been a very easy relationship with no drama. They enjoyed each other's company and liked the same things. Then six months ago she'd been offered the chance to run a hairdressing salon at a big glitzy hotel in Dubai.

The salon she had run in Birmingham city centre was struggling. She'd had to let valued staff go. She'd cut back on the cleaning and the number of towels they used. She hated cutting corners but she had no choice. People just weren't spending the money any more. They were going three months, even longer, without having their colour done, or doing it themselves at home. She was worried that the shop was going to go under. Then the opportunity of a lifetime had come along. Craig had had no second thoughts.

'You have to take it,' he told her. 'You hate your job at the moment. It's depressing. Dubai will be an awesome chance for you.'

Michelle and Craig were sensible enough to realise that their relationship wouldn't survive the separation. Neither of them wanted the pressure or the guilt of trying to maintain it in the long term.

'I don't want you to get out there and feel you can't have fun,' Craig told her.

'And I don't want you to mope around because I'm not there,' said Michelle.

So they agreed to part, but as friends. He drove her to the airport. She hugged him tight at the departure gate, and cried a bit, but he could tell she was excited about her new life. They'd agreed he would go out there at Christmas if neither of them had found someone else. Neither of them had so far, but Craig didn't think he would go. Long-distance relationships never worked. He'd seen the pictures she'd posted on Facebook and it felt as if he was looking at a stranger. They went on Skype from time to time too, but he found it upsetting. It just reminded him of what he was missing.

He'd been too caught up with the investigation to find anyone else. His mates egged him on when they went to the pub in Everdene for a drink. They thought he should find someone new, but he didn't want to force it. He wasn't one for one-night stands, not like some of his friends who went out with a different girl every time they came down to Devon. Maybe this weekend he should start to have a look round, he thought.

Not tonight, though. He wanted to wind down and get a decent night's sleep so that he could make the most of the weekend. Craig watched the waves roll in towards the shore. There would be plenty of time for pulling. He had the whole week, after all.

At half past nine, there was a bang on Jenna's door. It was so loud that she jumped off the bed, her heart thumping. She realised she had fallen asleep. She did that a lot these days. Being asleep was so much better than being awake. Her mouth went dry with fear. The knock came again, even louder. She thought about pretending that she wasn't in.

'Oi!' There was a shout from the other side of the door. She knew that voice only too well. 'I know you're in there. Open up.'

The landlord probably did know she was in

there. He had spies everywhere. She didn't trust any of the other tenants in the house.

'OK!' she called out, and hated how weedy her voice sounded.

She opened the door. The Prof was standing there. They called him The Prof because of his thick, black-rimmed glasses. Not because he was clever, unless you counted ripping desperate people off as clever. He was wearing a grubby white shirt, jeans and scuffed black slip-on shoes. Anyone would think he was on the breadline too.

'You got something for me?' He wandered in as if he owned the place. Which – technically – he did, but it was her room. He should respect her privacy.

Jenna swallowed hard.

'I'm really sorry,' she stammered. 'My boss wouldn't pay me. I haven't got the rent money. I'll get it for you by Monday. I promise.'

He made a clicking noise with his tongue behind his teeth.

'You're already behind. I'm going to have to start charging you interest.'

'I can't afford to pay you interest. I can't afford the rent as it is.'

He shrugged.

'It's not my problem.'

He walked over towards the window and looked around, then nodded.

'It's a big room, this. Too big for one. I could probably get a family in here. Not waste it on someone who won't pay up.'

He was threatening her, Jenna realised. How did he expect her to find the money? There was no point in asking him for sympathy. Men like him didn't care. How did he sleep at night, she wondered? Better than she did, probably.

She looked at him, and her stomach turned. He must rake in a fortune with all the money he took. What did he spend it on? He certainly didn't spend it on his clothes, or his hair, which needed a good cut, not to mention a wash. Or his car either – she'd seen him drive round in a battered old Ford Mondeo. She wondered where he lived, and if he had a wife, or any kids. She pitied them if he did.

Sometimes Jenna wondered if there were any decent men in the world.

He was walking towards her wardrobe, opening it up, looking through her stuff with that stupid grin on his face.

'Get out of my wardrobe,' Jenna told him.

He looked up. His hands were mauling her clothes, all the vintage dresses she'd bought in charity shops and at jumble sales and from

29

eBay. 'Just seeing if there's anything I could take instead of cash . . .'

She stepped towards him.

'There isn't anything. I've told you. I'll get the rent money.'

He raised an eyebrow.

'Yeah?' He looked her up and down. She shuddered as she felt his gaze undress her. She knew what he was thinking. She folded her arms across her chest. She didn't have to take this unspoken threat. He was a bully.

'Where do you get off, treating people like this?'

The Prof took a step back, surprised by her outburst.

'Like what?'

'Bullying them. Not just me, either. I've seen you bully that woman downstairs – the one with the baby. Does it make you feel good?'

He scowled, slamming the wardrobe door shut.

'All I want is what's owed to me. Nothing wrong with that.'

He came towards her with a smile. He reached out his hand and ran the back of his fingers down her cheek. His breath was stale and sour.

'Get me the rent. By Monday. And if I were you, I'd keep your opinions to yourself.'

Jenna jerked her head away. She could see that she'd rattled him. Something she'd said had touched a nerve. At least he hadn't mentioned interest. Even so, she still didn't have the rent. She hadn't got anything to sell. No jewellery, no nice watch, no computer, fancy phone or iPod. Those had all gone ages ago. At least she'd bought herself some time, though.

He looked at her steadily. She could see the stubble starting to poke through on his chin.

'I'll be back first thing on Monday.'

She thought he was probably enjoying torturing her. It's not as if he needed the money that much. He owned several houses around the town. He must be coining in thousands a week. He could afford to wait. If she pointed out that fact, she knew what he'd say. 'If I let you get away with it, they'll all want to pay late.'

At last he left the room. Jenna hadn't thought that she was going to get rid of him that easily, but maybe he had someone else to pick on. Her landlord was scum. He wasn't the only one of his kind around, though. There were quite a few 'entrepreneurs' in Tawcombe who'd bought up the big old Victorian houses that had been so splendid in their heyday. Especially now the town was a run-down seaside resort filled with unemployed and disillusioned people with no hope of escape. The landlords slapped up chipboard walls and cheap kitchens and crammed in as many tenants as they could find.

Jenna certainly wasn't the only person struggling. There were no decent jobs out here in the sticks. You could pick up casual work during the summer season if you were lucky, but there was slim chance of a proper career. She'd wanted to go to college but her mum had just laughed. She'd refused to support Jenna while she studied.

'Cheers for that, Mum,' she thought bitterly, though she shouldn't have been surprised. Her mum had never gone out of her way to help her with anything. Jenna had thought she'd be able to make a better life for herself on her own, but her plan had backfired big time. She was worse off now than she'd ever been, but no way was she going to go crawling back home. She knew she could just step outside and get on the bus that would take her two miles up the road to the estate where her mum lived, but she couldn't bear the thought of the look on her mum's face.

'Look what the cat's brought in,' she could hear her mother saying gleefully.

Never, thought Jenna. I'm never going back there. Instead, she had to find nearly four hundred quid by Monday morning, or she'd be out on the pavement surrounded by what little she had left.

Her landlord, The Prof, didn't make idle threats. She knew that for certain.

When night had fallen, the beach was wrapped in a soft navy-blue blanket spattered with stars. Craig unrolled his sleeping bag and curled up on one of the bunks in the beach hut, leaving the door slightly open. It was unlikely that anyone would try to get in, and he loved to go to sleep with the sound of the waves in the background. It was so soothing, more soothing than any lullaby. He loved the sound of the constant 'shushing' as the tide went in and out.

He checked the weather forecast on his phone before he fell asleep. Tomorrow was set fair. He'd get up early and hit the surf before anyone else.

Two minutes after his head hit the pillow, Craig was asleep.

*

Jenna was still wide awake at midnight. Her room was stifling, but if she opened her window the noise came in from outside the pub opposite. Her mind was whirling as she thought about the unfairness of the day. The full weight of being sacked was gradually beginning to hit her. Not only did she not have the money for the rent – her immediate problem – but what was she going to live on?

As she closed her eyes and tried to shut out the laughter of the pub-goers, her mind began to wander. What was the point of playing by the rules? It didn't seem to get you anywhere. The people she knew who'd done best in life, like The Prof, didn't seem to bother. Her family had never played it straight, any of them. They were on to every scam going, and they were all as happy as Larry. If you played it straight, it seemed as if you just sank to the bottom.

How was she going to get out of this trap? There would be no work going in Tawcombe for the rest of the summer. All the jobs were already taken. Maybe she could move to a bigger place? Bamford was the nearest big town, but she couldn't see a life for herself there. She didn't know anyone, for a start. Or a bigger city? Plymouth? Exeter? The thought of that terrified her. She'd only really known Tawcombe her whole life.

Jenna sighed. She was stuck here. She couldn't even afford a lottery ticket.

She turned onto her side and curled her legs up, tucking herself into a ball. All she could think about was The Prof's face on Monday morning. She bet he was hoping she wouldn't have the money. She was sure he enjoyed kicking people out of his scuzzy rooms so that he could lure someone else in and get the deposit from them.

Even if she found a job tomorrow morning, she couldn't get the money she needed in time. Nobody would pay her in advance. There were girls she knew who would know how to get that kind of money quickly. In a seaside town, there were always ways that you could supplement your income. Jenna wasn't going to take that path. Once you got into that, there was no way out. Anyway, the thought made her skin crawl. If she'd wanted to sell herself, she'd have made a deal with The Prof already . . .

As she felt the music from the pub pound through her body, she began to turn over possibilities in her mind.

Five minutes later, Jenna sat up as an idea occurred to her. Her heart thumped. Was it crazy? It seemed so simple. Of course it was wrong, but in the grand scheme of 'wrong', it was way down the scale. There were far, far worse things she could do.

She asked herself which was better – to be straight and penniless, or crooked and in the black, as far as money was concerned? She'd spent enough time already being the former, and it had nothing to recommend it. She'd always had a clear conscience, but you couldn't eat a strong set of moral values.

The more she thought about it, the more enticing her idea became.

As she went over the details and eventually drifted off to sleep, she told herself she only had to do it once, just once, until she got herself back on her feet.

Chapter Four

There was nothing more perfect than waking up by the sea and watching the sunrise.

Every time he saw it, Craig couldn't believe how lucky he was. By six o'clock in the morning, the copper from the Midlands was walking towards the sea with his surfboard tucked under his arms, his footprints in the damp sand the first of the day. He reached the water's edge.

The white frill of surf had looked like nothing from the hut, but once he got up close he realised the waves were pretty big. He ran straight into the water without stopping. His breath was taken away for a split second by the cold, but he carried on, paddling out behind the waves.

He surfed for nearly an hour. Craig was no expert and he envied the surfers who cut through the water with grace and elegance, as if they were at one with the waves. He knew that came with years of practice. These guys were devoted. They surfed every day, in all conditions. They were fanatics.

He'd heard their tales in the bar often enough. They told him about the surfing hot spots as far away as Hawaii, India and Australia, and their stories inspired him. He admired their devil-may-care attitude to life. They lived to surf. That was it. They picked up work when they could, where they could. They didn't worry about anything else. They had no responsibilities.

That kind of mindset didn't really suit him, being in the police. Until recently, Craig figured he had the best of both worlds. Where were these guys going to be in their old age? None of them would have a pension, just their memories. It was only now that he'd started to have doubts, to begin thinking differently, that he wondered about whether he'd really got it right.

Craig had given everything to his career. He loved his home town, and he'd wanted to contribute to its future. He wanted to make it a safe place, to protect his fellow townspeople from harm, to give them hope. Someone had once given him hope, after all, which was why he was lucky enough to be here now, enjoying the crystal-clear water.

By the time he got back to the beach hut with his surfboard, the early-morning sun had nearly dried him off after his dip in the sea. He pulled on his jeans and walked up the beach to the café in the arcade, taking a table outside. He ordered a surfer's breakfast of bacon, sausage, egg, mushrooms, tomato, beans, hash browns, toast and a pot of tea.

A guy he knew vaguely, Rusty, pulled up a chair next to him and sat down. That was the great thing about Everdene. You didn't see someone for months, but when you bumped into them, it was as if you'd seen them yesterday.

'Hey, buddy, how's it going?'

Rusty was from South Africa and was a photographer. He took pictures of the sea, blew them up onto canvas and sold them out of a camper van on the front. The tourists loved these shots, which funded Rusty's lifestyle. He didn't have to answer to anyone. He'd helped Craig out when he'd started surfing last summer. And Craig knew he would never be as good as Rusty could be in the water.

'Good, thanks,' replied Craig. 'Though I've had a rough time of it the past few weeks.'

He didn't know if Rusty would even remember he was a copper.

Rusty nodded. He looked up at the sky. 'Bad times, man.'

His hair was bleached blond by the sun. His skin was tanned, and his bright blue eyes shone out. Craig felt a twinge of envy at his lifestyle. Rusty would never have experienced the stress that Craig went through on a daily basis because of his job. The dryness in your mouth because you didn't know how things were going to turn out, or whether you were going to make the right decisions. And even if you did, whether you were going to make a difference.

And even if you did make a difference, whether it was then going to backfire.

Craig sighed. He didn't want to turn into a cliché of the disillusioned cop.

'So what have you been up to?' he asked.

Rusty took a tiny roll-up cigarette out of a tin in his pocket and lit it. He took a drag, sucked in the smoke, then blew it in a thin stream up in the air. Then he began to tell Craig what he'd been doing. He'd spent two months in Goa, then a month in Ireland, playing at festivals with some friends who had a band. Now he was back in Everdene to spend August teaching surfing to the tourists until the days grew short.

Craig put his head back and let the sun warm up the skin on his face as he listened. Rusty's life was as far away from his own as you could get. Every minute of Craig's life was accounted for. He didn't have a choice from the second he woke up.

Did he envy Rusty? He had very little, just his camper van, his surfboard and some worn and faded clothes, but he took opportunities as they presented themselves. Craig thought of his one-bedroomed apartment by the waterfront. The furniture he'd filled it with was all bought and paid for. He had a car, a wardrobe full of clothes and a top-of-the-range entertainment system. They were all the rewards of a tough job. Yet somehow the thought that nothing was going to change was constantly nagging at him. In the future, Craig would get a promotion, then probably a wife and kids, then maybe a house. There was nothing wrong with any of that, but would he ever see the world, like Rusty? Would he ever wake up in the morning and think, 'What now? Where next?' Who knew?

Even when he was down here at Everdene, he knew he was on borrowed time. It wouldn't be long before it was time to get back into the car and drive up the motorway. Then he would have to get back into his uniform and clock on. He'd be out in his police squad car, patrolling the streets, never knowing how much trouble the day was going to bring. He rarely came home feeling he'd done a good job. It wasn't that he was shocked by what people did, far from it. It was because he knew why they did it. The saying, 'There but for the grace of God go I' was often in his thoughts.

Next morning, Jenna woke at seven and listened to the sound of seagulls circling. She knew they would be feasting on the packets of leftover chips and kebabs dropped in the streets. They were scavengers to the end, those seagulls. She lay for a moment looking at the ceiling. There was a huge brown stain in the middle of it that seemed to bulge. She lived in fear of the roof caving in, imagining the bloke upstairs falling through the floor and landing on top of her, leaving a man-shaped hole.

She gave herself five minutes to decide whether she was going to go through with her plan. Even though it would mean she had failed. She had been so determined to prove herself.

'You think you're better than I am, don't you?' This had been her mother's parting shot.

'Yes, I do,' Jenna had told her, and her mum had just laughed. She could hear the cackle now, fuelled by fags and cheap bottles of supermarket own-brand vodka. Her mother's bloke went and bought a bottle of vodka every morning from the corner shop, and by four o'clock in the afternoon the pair of them would have polished it off, just in time to head to the pub.

Of course she thought she was better than that.

Jenna had dreamed that, if she got away from the grimy house where she had been brought up, she could make something of herself. She had to escape the lazy, drunken woman who had given birth to her and four other kids. Her Mum had never been a proper mother to any of them. If anything, they had to look after her. There were days when Jenna hadn't gone to school because her mum was so drunk that she was scared to leave her.

Jenna could remember going back to her friends' houses sometimes. She had looked on, wide-eyed, as their mothers fussed over them, made them tea and asked about their day. She had sat in the bedrooms of her schoolfriends, with their crisply ironed duvet covers and matching curtains, and fluffy dressing gowns and slippers. They had clean towels hanging in the bathroom and toilet paper on a holder. There were proper mealtimes when the whole family sat round the table. They had fathers who came home and hugged them. They had fathers who would never raise a voice, let alone a hand, to their wife or kids.

Jenna wasn't jealous, but she never invited anyone back to her house. She would have been too ashamed because their house was a hovel. The tiny front yard was studded with dog turds that baked hard in the sun or turned to mush in the rain. Sometimes, Jenna cleared them up but she ended up gagging. Inside the house, the lounge was covered in dog hairs and the wallpaper had been scratched off the wall. Every surface in the kitchen was covered in dirty cups and plates, cereal boxes and take-away cartons. There were empty bottles every-where, but no glasses. Her mum just poured vodka straight into a can of 7Up and glugged it. In the hall, there were tins of dog food up-ended straight onto the floor. Her mum argued that the dogs only took two seconds to eat it, because they were always starving, so what was the point of dirtying a dish?

Whatever happened, Jenna wasn't going back there.

She blinked back the familiar tears. It was up to her now. She had no one else, and that was how she liked it – even though it was hard. She forced herself to get out of bed. She could lie there all day, but then she would be just like her mother. She had to keep going, even though she knew that what she was about to do was wrong.

Jenna got herself dressed – before she could change her mind. She put on a bikini, then chose a dress. She didn't want to stand out, so she picked out one with a simple white halter neck. In a bag, she put a towel, some suncream, a bottle of water and a book. She tied her hair in a high ponytail and finished off the look with a pair of sunglasses and some flip-flops decorated with big flowers.

As she left the house, she looked like any normal young girl about to spend a day on the beach.

Jenna had just enough money for the bus fare to Everdene. It was only five miles away, but it might as well have been a thousand. Her heart lifted every time she went down the hill to-wards the bay. It was as unlike Tawcombe as you could get. Everywhere you looked there was beauty, from the rolling hills to the sea to the sun on the distant horizon. There were shades of green and blue and shimmering gold.

She'd come here before – sometimes with her mates. They ate chips on the beach, washed down with bottles of cider, and got the late bus back. They never went in the sea. That was for tourists and surfers. As far as Jenna was concerned, the sea might look nice – but it was cold and wet.

She got off the bus in the centre of the village where the traffic was insane. On a hot day, in the height of summer, you had to find a parking space by nine o'clock or you had no hope. The pavements were crowded with people heading to the beach, lugging their beach bags, buckets, spades and body boards. It was a nightmare getting through, dodging push-chairs and dogs on leads, but Jenna kept her head down and pushed on. In the end, she walked in the road, because it was easier. The traffic was so slow that she was unlikely to get run over. She didn't think about what she was going to do. She had no choice, she told herself – over and over.

She passed the Ship Aground, the pub in the middle of Everdene where everyone hung out. There was a huge poster outside, advertising their end-of-season pop-singing competition. The first prize was a hundred pounds. For a moment, Jenna hesitated. Her friends were always trying to persuade her to enter competitions like this. They were always telling her she had an amazing voice, but she didn't have the confidence. It was one thing mucking about in the ice-cream kiosk, but it was quite another walking out on stage.

Anyway, even if she did enter, and even if she won, what then? She'd have a hundred quid in her pocket, but that wasn't enough to live on or to pay the rent she owed. Her current plan was going to make her more money. She turned away and walked on.

As she passed the coffee shop in the arcade at the top of the beach, she realised that she hadn't eaten or drunk anything since she'd left the ice-cream kiosk yesterday afternoon. She pulled out the last of her change and estimated she had enough for a cup of tea. With three sugars in it, it might keep her going for a while. She ducked inside and ordered a takeaway cup. As she paid and turned to leave, she was just taking off the plastic lid when she bumped straight into a man heading for the counter.

Luckily she hadn't been holding the cup close to her, or it would have spilled all down her front. Instead, it went all over the floor.

'Oh my God, I'm so sorry.' The man put

47

out his hand and touched her arm. 'Are you OK?'

'I'm fine,' said Jenna, looking up, right into the most incredible eyes. Eyes that were silver-grey, with the longest lashes she had ever seen on a man – and set in a kind face, too.

'I wasn't looking where I was going . . .'

'Neither was I.' She managed a laugh. Wow! This guy was really good-looking, she thought. There were always a lot of good-looking guys in Everdene, but he was even hotter than most. He had dark curly hair, cropped close, and was lean and muscular in his T-shirt and faded jeans.

'Let me get you another.' He looked at her, his dark brows meeting in a frown. 'Seriously. Go and sit down and I'll bring you one over.'

Jenna bit her lip, thinking how wonderful it would be to sit down while he brought her a fresh drink. Then she remembered what she was doing here, and realised that today of all days she didn't want to bring attention to herself. The last thing she needed was to strike up conversation with a handsome stranger who might remember her.

'It's OK. It's fine. I'm in a hurry. Honestly. I have to go.'

She smiled and walked away as quickly as she

could, throwing her empty cup into the nearest bin.

Eventually Jenna made it onto the sand. The tide was in, which meant at the moment there was little room for people to set up camp. As the sea inched out again, the visitors began to spread out their rugs, putting up their wind-breaks and laying out all the things they needed for the day. The sun grew ever more sparkling, welcoming the crowds with its rays.

Jenna spread out her towel at the bottom of the bank beneath the beach huts. She'd chosen her pitch carefully. She wanted to be on the edge of the crowds, so she could watch, but she didn't want to stand out. Everyone was so busy having a good time that they weren't going to notice her.

Chapter Five

Craig noticed Jenna straight away.

She was the girl he'd bumped into at the coffee shop. She was sitting at the bottom of the bank outside his beach hut. She looked as if she'd stepped out of a 1950s film set, with her curves and her high ponytail and her retro dress. She really was very pretty, and he wondered why she was here on her own. Maybe she was waiting for her mates, or her boyfriend? Maybe that was why she hadn't let him buy her a drink, because there was another bloke in the picture.

Craig told himself to stop staring but he wasn't sure what else to do. There was certainly no point in trying to surf while the beach was this busy. Even though there were supposed to be separate areas for surfers and swimmers, Craig could see it was chaos in the water. He wasn't a good enough surfer to avoid hitting someone if they got in his way. He'd wait until later this evening, when the crowds had gone. The waves would still be good. In the meantime, he put up his striped deckchair in front of the hut and sat watching all the people on the beach. He wondered who they were and where they had come from as little dramas unfolded. A teenage boy fussed over his gran, making sure she was comfortable. Two small toddlers fought over a spade until their mother intervened. A young couple stretched out on a rug together, sharing the headphones on an iPod.

His eyes kept straying back to the girl with the ponytail. She was still on her own. Maybe he should go and talk to her, or offer her another drink? If his friends were here, he knew they would be encouraging him, but without them he felt shy. Maybe she wanted to be on her own and didn't want company? Craig decided in the end he would leave her alone. He picked up his book instead and started to read.

Jenna spread her things out around her, then rubbed some suncream on her arms and the back of her neck. She didn't want to burn in the heat of the sun. From behind her sunglasses, she examined all the groups of people around her. She made sure she knew exactly who was in each group, and how the dynamics worked. Small families with toddlers would be the best target. The parents of small children were always distracted.

Jenna had never stolen anything in her life before, but she knew plenty of people who had. Members of her family were always coming home with knocked-off gear or things that had 'fallen off the back of a lorry'. Her mum was always sticking stuff in her pocket when she was out shopping. It was a way of life for them, but Jenna hadn't had to stoop that low before.

She felt sick that it had come to this, but she was desperate. Her mum's words came back to her time and again. 'You're no better than the rest of us.' Well, maybe not, but at least she'd had a go at getting out there and trying to make a better life for herself. Anyway, she reminded herself, this was a one-off. She told herself she was only getting back what had been stolen from her a couple of weeks ago. She knew deep down that was no excuse, of course, but she didn't know what else to do. It was either this or be thrown out of her room by The Prof on Monday.

Jenna looked around the beach again. She knew all the rules of pickpocketing. When you came from the kind of family she did, you picked up these things along the way. She knew how to identify an easy victim, a 'mark', and the best conditions to steal from them. You had to wait until they were off their guard and weren't paying attention. The beach was perfect for that, because people were concentrating so hard on having a good time that they forgot to look after their valuables. Of course, it was better to have an accomplice, a partner in crime, but that was out of the question. Jenna could hardly have asked one of her mates to come and help her.

She decided to try the ice-cream queue first. There were three vans parked along the beach, and the searing heat meant that the lines outside them were already long. She waited nearby until she saw a harassed-looking father join the queue with two small children in tow. She slipped in behind him, guessing it was going to be at least ten minutes before they got to the window. By then, everyone would be more hot and bothered than ever.

She examined her target. She could see his wallet in the back pocket of his shorts. He was doing his best to control his two children, who were bawling in fury that their ice cream wasn't coming sooner. When he bent down to tell off one of them, she whisked the wallet out of his pocket and into her own.

Before the children had stopped arguing, she

left the queue. Anyone would think she was just bored with waiting. She didn't wait to see the man's reaction when he discovered his loss. At first he would assume he had dropped his wallet on the walk over, or that he'd forgotten to put it in his pocket. It would probably be at least twenty minutes before he figured out he'd been pickpocketed, and by then he wouldn't be sure where it had happened. Jenna would be long gone.

Her heart was hammering and her mouth was dry as she made her way back to her towel. She felt slightly sick, too, although she wasn't sure whether that was a combination of the heat and the fact that she still hadn't eaten. She opened the wallet, pulled out three twenty-pound notes and a crumpled fiver and put them in her bag. All she had to do now was get rid of the evidence. She walked a couple of hundred yards back up the beach to where six big black bins were regularly emptied throughout the day. She lifted the lid, recoiling slightly from the stench of chip wrappers and dirty nappies baking in the sunshine, and dropped the wallet in. She wasn't going to touch the credit cards. That wasn't her level of crime at all, although she knew people who would have found them useful.

So far, so good, she thought. She didn't want to think about whether she'd ruined the family's day out. Feeling guilty was not going to help with the task in hand. She went back to her blanket for a few minutes and waited until her heart had stopped hammering. Then she decided to head up the beach in the other direction. She'd spotted a young couple walking down to the water, hand in hand. The girl had very carefully placed her handbag under a towel before they left, as if that was going to fool anyone. Some people, thought Jenna, were very stupid.

Craig woke with a start, realising he'd fallen asleep in the heat of the midday sun. There was sweat trickling down his forehead, and he was dying of thirst. He should probably go back into the hut, into the shade. He sat up and glanced around, mostly to see if anyone had spotted him dribbling while he was asleep. He looked down to the bottom of the bank to see if the girl with the ponytail was still there, but her towel was empty. Her stuff was still there, though, so she had to be around.

He scanned the crowds, looking for her, and thought he could spot her ponytail and white dress further up the beach. He reached down for the pair of binoculars he kept by him. There were always interesting things to look at – a passing ship, a hang-glider, a bird of prey – and it also meant he could keep an eye on the surfing conditions when the tide was out. At last, he caught sight of the girl through the lenses. Was he being a bit of a stalker? Surely it wasn't normal, to spy on someone like this, but the girl had fascinated him. He watched her as she walked further up the beach.

A few moments later, Craig couldn't believe his eyes as she approached someone's empty rug, reached under a towel, found a bag and took out a purse, all in one fluid movement that took less than five seconds. Then she walked calmly away, back up the beach towards him.

He didn't know why he was so shocked. After all, he was used to this sort of behaviour. He arrested people like this girl every day of the week in the town centre. Admittedly, they usually worked in gangs rather than on their own. There would be one on lookout, and one causing a distraction. Maybe he was shocked because he viewed Everdene as an escape. He'd built it up in his mind as some sort of romantic hideaway where nothing bad ever happened, but of course it did. A crowded beach was the perfect place for a petty thief.

He followed her progress back up the beach. He watched her take money out of the purse, stuff the notes in her pocket, then ditch the purse in the bins as she walked past. His heart sank as he realised that this meant she was definitely guilty, although if he was going to confront her he needed proof.

He felt a sour taste in his mouth. He didn't want to deal with this, but now that he had seen it happen, he couldn't ignore it, even if he was off duty. Of course, he could just turn a blind eye, but that wasn't in Craig's nature. He'd never been one to stand by and let people do wrong. Even after what had happened to him lately, he was still a policeman, first and foremost.

Or maybe he'd just imagined what had happened. It was certainly hot enough to make you see things, and the heat of the sun made everything hazy. He'd had a beer as well, from the fridge, which might have impaired his judgement. Maybe he should just carry on reading. It was too beautiful a day for trouble. Then he sighed and picked up his binoculars. He would sit and watch her to see what she did next. If she just sat on her towel and did nothing else, he decided, he would give her the benefit of the doubt and leave her alone.

Jenna drank half a bottle of water and lay back down in the sun. She couldn't believe how easy it had been. She mustn't get carried away, though. Word might start spreading on the beach. She would just do one more today, then go to the other beach around the point tomorrow. One thing she had learned from her family as she grew up was never go back to the scene of the crime.

The other thing she knew was that even if someone did call the police, they wouldn't come out. They weren't going to bother to respond to a crime where the victims had been stupid enough to leave their stuff unattended. On a busy Saturday in the summer, when they were already understaffed, there were far more important things they could be dealing with.

She just had to hold her nerve. There was over a mile of beach to choose from. She was anonymous. Everyone looked right through her. If Jenna needed proof that she was a nobody, this was it. She sat up again. The heat was intense, as if the sun was burning a hole in the sky. It was hard to look at the sea without squinting. The light reflecting off the water was almost white.

One more, Jenna decided. She'd spotted a family. Earlier she'd seen the dad take his wallet out and give the three kids money for ice creams. They looked well off. They had all the kit. UV tents and thick, plush beach towels and a sleek spaniel on a lead, as well as a cool box brimming with all manner of treats. Jenna's stomach rumbled and she realised that she still hadn't eaten anything. She watched as the mother opened the cool box and rummaged inside, handing out drinks.

She wondered if they knew how lucky they were. She'd never been on holiday. 'What do you want to go on holiday for?' her mum had asked. 'We live by the sea. People pay to come here. Why would we want to pay to go somewhere else?'

Jenna knew she shouldn't sit there feeling sorry for herself to justify her actions. This wasn't about self-pity, or feeling bitter. This was about survival. Besides, thought Jenna, this family could definitely afford to lose a few quid. She watched while the mother zipped up the children's wetsuits and gathered up the towels to take down to the water, then applied suncream to the backs of their necks. The dad shoved his wallet in the cool box, obviously thinking that no one would look in there for something to steal. She shook her head in disbelief.

The tide was at its lowest, so the family had a long way to walk to get to the sea. She watched until they were three-quarters of the way there, then made her way over to their encampment. She plonked herself casually down on the rug, then lifted the cool-box lid. She rummaged about inside, looking for all the world like a young girl finding the best thing to eat.

She pulled out an egg roll, oozing with mayonnaise, and a giant chocolate-chip cookie. She looked down to the shoreline where the family had reached the water. It would take them at least ten minutes to walk back, even if they remembered that they had forgotten something vital. She devoured the roll, then rifled through the wallet as she munched on the biscuit. There was over a hundred quid in there. Three credit cards. A photo of the family, the kids in posh uniforms outside a massive house. For some reason this made her feel better. They weren't going to miss the money.

She might as well take the whole lot. There was no point in leaving them any. They were obviously loaded. The man would be furious for about an hour, then he'd go to the cashpoint and get some more money. It was no big deal. It was his own fault for leaving his wallet un-attended. She folded up the notes and stuffed them in her pocket, then put the lid back on the cool box. She felt slightly sick from eating so fast in the heat of the sun. Then she stood up and walked away.

Chapter Six

Craig's heart was thumping, which was crazy. This wasn't some stake-out on a dodgy estate where things could go badly if he made the wrong move. So why was he worried? He should just march over, collar the girl and make people aware that this kind of crime could happen, even somewhere as carefree as Everdene. That might make them take more care of their valuables.

Something was stopping him, though. He'd felt drawn to the girl the moment he had bumped into her in the café. He wanted to know why she was doing this. Instinct told him this wasn't her usual behaviour. She didn't have the air of a hardened pickpocket, and the way she had taken food out of the cool box told him she was hungry. Although being hungry didn't excuse what she was doing, far from it.

Craig knew that if his mates were here they wouldn't give her a chance, and that they'd call him soft. Well, maybe he was soft, softer than he admitted even to himself. In fact, he had to face up to it now. He'd lost his killer instinct. He'd been dragged over the coals, and even though he'd been cleared of blame, the experience had soured him. Where once he had felt it was his duty to see justice done, now he was asking himself questions. And a good cop shouldn't hesitate.

He sighed, put down his binoculars and got out of his deckchair. He could see her without them now, weaving her way among the holidaymakers back to her towel. He paused for a moment, and watched as she sat down, then put her head in her hands. He could see by her body language that she felt guilty. Her shoulders were hunched and she moved slowly as she started gathering her things up ready to leave. Smart move, thought Craig, because it was about time she moved on. That last family looked as if they would cause a fuss, and it would be better for her if she wasn't around when they raised the alarm.

He watched as she stuffed the last of her things in her bag and stood up. He walked down the last few feet of the bank and made his way towards her as she moved off. He fell into step beside her and put a hand on her arm.

'Hey,' he said, not loudly, as he didn't want to cause alarm. She stopped.

'What?' She looked straight at him. There was a moment of confusion, then she recognised him. 'You were in the café.'

'I saw what you did,' he told her.

'What?' she repeated, frowning this time, and he saw that her eyes were amber speckled with gold. 'Spilled my tea, you mean?'

For a moment, in the heat of the sun, he doubted himself again. He felt awkward. This was far more difficult than an arrest, when he was in uniform. He wasn't quite sure what to say.

'No. I saw you nick that wallet out of the cool box. And take that purse out of that woman's handbag earlier.' He pointed back down the beach.

She shook her head. 'I don't know what you're talking about.'

She moved away and carried on walking. He walked beside her.

'I've got photos.'

She hesitated for a moment. 'Of what?'

'Good enough evidence for a court of law.'

She turned on him. 'Go and hassle someone else, will you? You're being weird.'

'I should have you arrested.'

'I should have *you* arrested. You've been

64

following me since this morning, taking pictures. That's stalking.'

He was impressed by the way she stood her ground. On the surface, she seemed defiant. A passer-by would believe her innocence, but Craig had been trained to read body language. Her fists were clenched, and she refused to make eye contact. He was going to have to be more forceful to get her to admit her guilt. Yet somehow his heart wasn't in it.

Maybe he should just let her go and be done with it. Thinking she had been caught would probably put her off doing it again, and this was supposed to be his week off. He just wanted to chill and get things straight in his head. This was like being back at work, if not worse. All he really wanted to do was sit back down and have a beer and maybe fall asleep again.

Craig nearly gave up and let her go, but something inside him wanted to know more about her. He wanted to know why she was on the beach nicking money. He never had time, when he arrested people, to go into the whys and wherefores, and he was interested.

'I don't want to make a big scene,' he told her. 'But I can't just let you walk off with all that money.'

She spread her hands, laughing. 'There is no

money. I haven't even got enough for an ice cream.'

He held her gaze.

'Open your bag. Let me have a look.'

'Leave me alone. Or I'm going to call for help.'

He looked around and then took his wallet out of his shorts. 'You better take a look at this.'

He flipped it open and showed her his police identification.

She stared at it for a good five seconds before she finally dropped her eyes to the ground. She sighed and turned away.

'I didn't have any choice,' she said, her voice tight with tears.

'We all have a choice,' he replied. 'I've got a choice right now. I can take you into the nearest station. Or we can talk about it.'

'What are you, my counsellor, all of a sudden?' she asked, crossly.

He raised an eyebrow. 'Normal girls of your age don't come to the beach on their own and spend the day nicking money.'

'You think I don't know that?' She raised her voice, and he realised that people were looking.

'Look,' he said. 'I'm a cop. By rights it's my duty to turn you in. But I'm on holiday. I don't want a load of hassle.' He looked at her. She was staring down at the sand. The fight seemed to have gone out of her. 'And I bet you don't either.'

She looked up and put her hands on her hips. 'So what are you going to do? Give me some big lecture? It's not as if I don't know it's wrong.'

'So why did you do it?'

She stared at him. Her eyes were huge in her face. He reached out a hand and touched her arm.

'Come on. Come inside and have a drink. We can talk about it.'

Jenna stood there. She didn't know what to do. All she knew was that the heat was suddenly unbearable and she felt sick. She wasn't scared. She didn't feel like running away. In fact, she almost felt a sense of relief. Her future was now going to be out of her hands. Someone else was going to be in control.

She looked up at the bloke again. He was going to decide her fate. She didn't have to make the decisions any more. She couldn't read the expression in his silver-grey eyes. She'd expected harshness and accusation but they seemed almost understanding.

'Come on,' said the man, nodding his head up towards the faded blue beach hut behind him. 'We don't want to have this discussion in public.'

For a moment Jenna was tempted to run. She was wearing flip-flops, which were impossible to run in, but she could kick them off. How far would she get? Not far, she knew. And he looked fit.

She followed him obediently up the slope towards the beach hut. He had broad shoulders tapering down to a slender waist. He was wearing red surfing shorts decorated with flowers although there was nothing girly about him. He was lightly tanned, and his skin glistened where he'd put on suncream. Despite her heart thumping, she managed a smile to herself. Nice work, Jenna – you've been caught red-handed by the hottest cop you've ever seen.

Chapter Seven

Jenna followed her captor up to the beach hut. She could see where he'd been sitting, in a red and white striped deckchair. There were a couple of empty bottles of beer, and a pair of binoculars.

'I've been watching you all afternoon,' he said.

Jenna said nothing. She knew from experience that was the best policy. Don't confess or deny anything.

He led her into the hut. Inside it was surprisingly cool. He poured her a glass of water without asking, and she drank thirstily.

'So do you do this a lot?' he asked.

Whatever she said was going to sound like a line. If she told him this was the first time she had ever nicked anything, he would say, 'Of course it is', in that nasty voice coppers kept specially for such occasions.

'Easier than getting a job,' she told him defiantly.

'How much did you get?'

'I don't know . . .'

He held out his hand to take her bag. She had no choice but to give it to him.

'So,' she asked him. 'Where are your handcuffs? Are you going to march me back up the beach past everyone?'

He pulled out the money. When he saw how much there was, he raised his eyebrows.

'Quite a bit,' he said, and started to count it. Jenna felt sick with humiliation. Seeing all that money that belonged to other people made her feel even worse than she already did. She just wanted to lie down and curl up into a ball, then go to sleep for ever.

He was nodding as he counted.

'Two hundred and seventy-five quid,' he remarked. 'Beats working for a living, I suppose.'

His cool grey eyes stared at her.

'No,' she said. 'Actually, I'd much rather be working.' The stress of the last couple of days boiled up inside her. 'Do you think I want to do this? Do you think I felt good about myself, sitting there on the beach, looking for the people who I thought wouldn't miss the money?'

Suddenly her knees went weak and she saw black dots at the corners of her eyes. She swayed for a moment and shut her eyes. She was going to throw up. She looked around in a panic, her hand on her stomach.

'Here.' He grabbed the washing-up bowl from the sink and thrust it at her just in time. She took it from him and vomited, her cheeks burning. She wiped her mouth, sweat breaking out on her forehead. It didn't get any worse than this. Meeting a hot guy, then him catching you stealing, then puking up in front of him.

What a class act, Jenna thought. She couldn't look at the bloke. She wanted to crawl away into a corner and die.

'Sorry . . .' she managed at last.

'You've had too much sun,' he told her, and took away the bowl. 'Go into the bathroom and clean yourself up. There's mouthwash.'

She did as she was told. In the tiny bathroom she gripped the edge of the sink and looked at herself in the mirror. Her hair was plastered to her forehead and her cheeks were burning. Her head felt as if it was held in a vice. She felt too terrible to worry about what was going to happen to her. She washed her face with cold water, rinsed out her mouth and found the mouthwash. Then she ventured out again, not sure what was going to happen next.

*

While she was in the bathroom, Craig looked at the money and tried to decide what to do. He should turn her in, but what good would that do? She'd go up before the magistrate. Even if they were lenient she would have a record that would make sure no one gave her a job.

When she came back out she looked terrible. She was shivering, even though it was hot. He thought it was probably a mixture of sunstroke and shock. He went over to put the kettle on. What a cliché, thinking a nice cup of tea could solve anything, but it seemed the best thing to do.

She sat down on the settee without being asked, then leaned back and shut her eyes. Her hair was damp where she had washed her face.

'I'm Craig, by the way,' he told her. 'Do you want to tell me your name?'

'Jenna . . .' she replied, faintly. He thought she was telling the truth.

'OK, Jenna,' he replied, opening the cupboard to find the tea bags. 'What do you think we should do about this situation?'

She shrugged. 'You're the policeman.'

He lobbed a couple of tea bags into two mugs.

'Why?' he asked. 'It's a pretty rubbish thing to

do, don't you think? Nicking people's money when they've come for a day out on the beach?'

She stared into the middle of the room, sullen.

'Where do you suggest I go, then? Up to the hospital, where people are having a shit time anyway? So my nicking their money won't make any difference to how they feel?'

He had to hide a smile at her logic. He poured water onto the tea bags, got the milk out of the fridge and added a splash to each mug. He walked over and handed her one. She took it from him without a word of thanks, just held it between her knees, her shoulders hunched again. Her hair had come loose from its pony-tail, falling onto her shoulders, and he thought again how pretty she was.

'How about not doing it at all?' he asked.

She slammed her mug down on the coffee table in front of her.

'Those people aren't going to miss that money,' she told him. 'They're just here to have a good time. They haven't got a care in the world, any of them. I was watching. They've got everything they could possibly want.'

Craig looked at her. 'Does that make it right, then?'

'No, of course it doesn't,' she shot back. 'I

know it's wrong. I don't need you to judge me. You with your job, and your beach hut, and your surfboard, hanging out by the sea. You don't know what it's like, to have no hope, no money. Nothing. I've got nothing!' she shouted at him. 'I've got the clothes I'm standing up in, but that's it. I lost my job and my boss never gave me my wages. I owe my landlord four hundred quid, and if I don't get it, he's going to kick me out. Tell me what I was supposed to do, Mr Policeman?'

She spat the last few words out with real venom. Craig was silent for a moment.

'Actually,' he told her, 'I do know what it's like to have absolutely nothing.'

She gave a snort of disbelief. 'Yeah, right.'

'I was brought up on an estate on the out-skirts of the city. My brother was a drug dealer, but my mum thought the sun shone out of him because he brought her things. Things he'd nicked. She never took any notice of me. So I decided I'd start nicking things too.'

The girl looked up in surprise at this confession. Craig gave a wry smile. He didn't think he'd ever admitted this to anyone before. It wasn't something he was proud of.

'Lucky for me, there was a teacher at my school who could see I had potential. He gave me a really hard time. He went on and on at me until I realised he was right: that I would have more of a chance if I passed my exams. When I got my exam results, eight GCSEs, my mum didn't take any notice. She was too busy watching the big-screen telly that my brother had got her.'

Craig still remembered his anger now – the feeling of hopelessness, wondering what on earth was the point – and he'd thrown the letter with his results in the bin. His teacher had come to find him, told him how proud he was, showed him everything that piece of paper would allow him to do.

'Three weeks later, my brother got shot in a drive-by shooting and I decided to join the police. My mum never spoke to me again, because my brother had taught her to blame the cops for everything.' Craig paused for breath. The memory was still painful. 'So don't give me your sob story. I could have followed in my brother's footsteps. I had every opportunity, I can tell you. But I didn't.'

Jenna didn't say anything. She stared at the floor. Eventually she looked up.

'I'm sorry about your brother,' she said. 'But it's not that easy, you know. Just because you found a way out doesn't mean that we all can.'

Craig frowned. 'So that's it, is it? You feel justified?'

Jenna jumped to her feet. 'No. I never felt justified. I felt desperate.' Her amber eyes were flashing as she crossed the room to stand in front of him. 'How am I supposed to pay my rent? It's no good telling me to go to the council. He wants cash. Now.' She was trembling with fury. 'Of course, there's one way I could pay him. I know that. But I kind of thought nicking a few quid from people who wouldn't notice was a better way to go than sleeping with some sleazebag . . .'

'Hey, hey, hey.' Alarmed by her reaction, he went to put his arm round her shoulder. She shook it off.

'Just get off me.' She pulled away from him and threw her bag across the room so that its contents spilled on the floor. 'I'll leave it up to you to do what you think is best with the money.'

The next moment, she was gone. The door of the beach hut swung shut behind her. Craig stood in the middle of the room with no idea what to do. Going after her would do no good. He didn't have a solution to her problem. If he did, he would be running the country by now. There were thousands like her, stuck in a trap.

He saw them every day, saw the results of their desperation and what they did as a result. He'd made the classic mistake, of thinking that just because he had pulled himself up by his bootstraps, anyone could change their life for the better.

He went to the fridge and pulled out a beer. He took off the top with the opener someone had screwed to the wall and took a sip. It tasted bitter. He put the bottle down. Getting drunk was no solution when you felt bad. He saw the results of substance abuse every day. People who took drink and drugs to forget, not to have fun.

He walked over to the settee and sat down. So much for a quiet, relaxing week. Instead, what had happened today had brought everything into sharp focus, highlighting all of the things he felt unhappy about. He had, he knew, joined the police for all the right reasons, but now he wasn't sure he was doing the right thing any more. When he looked at people like Jenna and sympathised with their plight, how could he carry on? Maybe it was time for him to make a difference in some other way. Turning a blind eye today was one thing, but he couldn't do that when he went back to work.

The incident had only confirmed for him

what he already felt in his gut, that the day was coming closer and closer when he would have to walk away.

Chapter Eight

Jenna ran all the way back up the beach to the road. Running on the sand was hard work, and she was soon out of breath. She slowed down to a walk as she went through the village towards the bus stop. She passed the Ship Aground again, and saw the band bringing in the gear for that evening's singing competition. She stopped for a moment, wondering whether she had the nerve to enter.

'Don't be stupid, Jenna,' she told herself. 'You're not good enough.'

She remembered her birthday, a few years ago now. Everyone had piled round to her house, all her brothers and sisters and their mates and her mates. The house was heaving, the booze was flowing and the music was pumping. There was a real party atmosphere, even though she hadn't sent out any official invites. For once, the mood in the house was light. Even her mum was happy – she'd done herself up to the nines, and was dancing and laughing and flirting with all Jenna's brothers' mates.

Someone had brought round a karaoke machine. Nicked, no doubt, but everyone started to take it in turns to have a go. Jenna felt too shy at first, but her friends encouraged her. They'd heard her sing and they thought she was great. They weren't going to stop, so Jenna picked up the microphone.

She sang 'Beautiful' by Christina Aguilera. Everyone else had chosen upbeat singalong songs, from bands like the Spice Girls and Take That, so for a moment she felt awkward when she realised everyone had stopped talking and laughing, and was actually watching her. She wasn't note perfect, not by any means. Every time she made a mistake she cringed inside and wanted to run off, but she carried on. When the last note died away, there was silence. Then suddenly everyone broke into wild applause.

Jenna couldn't believe she'd actually done it, sung on her own in front of a roomful of people. It felt amazing. She felt . . . beautiful, just like in the song.

Then her mother had stepped in front of her, grabbed the microphone, put on another song – something rowdy and upbeat. In the blink of an eye she had the whole room singing along with her, cheering and clapping. Jenna was forgotten. Overshadowed. She'd felt invisible again. How could she have thought she was any good? Everyone was drunk. They were just playing along with her. The applause had been empty. They'd have clapped for anyone . . .

The memory burned inside her, and she turned away from the pub and headed to the bus stop. Five minutes later she was on the bus to Tawcombe, leaving Everdene and the horrors of the day behind her.

As soon as she got back to her house, she went into her room, shut the door and leaned against it. She felt numb, unsure whether to laugh or cry or just throw herself onto the bed and go to sleep. She wanted to block out everything that had happened in the past twenty-four hours. She wanted to block out the future, too. Just one more day and The Prof would be knocking on the door, an oily smile on his face, knowing full well she didn't have the rent.

She looked around at the shabby furniture and the few things she had that made the room her own. She wouldn't be sorry to leave. Her time here had not been happy. The other tenants in the house had been in no hurry to make friends. She had never felt comfortable bringing anyone back here. Her friends would have been shocked, even though they might not live in palaces themselves.

As she looked around, Jenna understood that she had no choice but to go back home. She would go now, tonight. She would save The Prof the pleasure of evicting her. She couldn't stand the thought of his face as he made her pack up her stuff. And this way, she wouldn't have to owe him the money. He might try to track her down and chase her for it, but at the end of the day how could you get money out of someone who didn't have any?

For the next half-hour, Jenna went through her wardrobe and her drawers, sorting out everything she wanted to take with her. Then she piled it all into two black bin bags. That was it, everything she had in the world. She put them by the door. She'd call a cab. Her mum would have to pay the fare when she got there.

She picked up the bags and stood in the doorway for a moment. So much for making her own way in the world. She'd reached rock bottom today. Her mum was so right. Of course she wasn't any better than any of them. She belonged right back there with the rest of her family. How could she possibly have imagined there was a better life out there?

She thought about Craig. Why couldn't she

have ended up with someone like him? Someone decent and honest who'd made his way in
the world, even though he'd had no better a
start than she had.

The door slammed shut behind her. She
stepped out into the street, blinking at the
early-evening sun that shone in her eyes, and
trailed up the road to find a taxi.

No one batted an eyelid when she walked
through the door. Her mum was lying on the
settee watching telly. She grumbled a bit when
Jenna asked for a fiver to pay the cab driver, but
she gave it to her.

'You're back, then?' she asked. 'You can't
have your room. Your brother's using it as an
office.'

'An office?' Jenna frowned.

'Yeah. He's set himself up in business. De-
livering pet food. He keeps it all in the garage.
He's doing all right for himself.'

Her mum sat up. Jenna looked at her more
closely.

'What?' her mum asked.

'Nothing. You look . . . different, that's all.'
She did. She looked slimmer, younger, not so
puffy. And she wasn't drunk. Usually by this

time on a Saturday she'd have started the second bottle of vodka.

'I've got a new bloke, haven't I?'

Jenna put down her bags and glanced around the room. Everything looked tidy. There were no dog hairs. There were no empty glasses, no ashtrays. In fact, her mum wasn't smoking.

'Have you given up the fags as well?' she asked.

'Most of the time,' her mum admitted. 'I have the odd sneaky one every now and again. I wouldn't want to be perfect, would I?' She grinned at Jenna, then looked away.

Jenna felt a lump in her throat. She turned away before her mum could see her tears and think she was soft. Instead, she lugged her bin bags upstairs and put them in her old room. All her stuff had gone, but she could sleep on the floor for the time being. Compared to her old flat, it would be luxury.

Her mum appeared behind her in the door-way.

'I'll give you a hand shifting his stuff out. Your brother can do his paperwork in the kitchen.'

'Thanks.'

Her mum traced the pattern of the carpet

with the toe of her shoe, then cleared her throat.

'I'm cooking a chilli tonight, if you want some. You can meet Arnie.'

Jenna looked out of the window onto the front garden that she'd stared out at so many times during her childhood. She noticed that the lawn had been cut, and there were two pots of flowers on either side of the front door. Whoever Arnie was, he'd certainly made some changes happen. She couldn't remember the last time her mum had cooked a proper meal.

'I'd love that,' she managed finally. 'But there's something I've got to do first. Can you lend me a tenner?'

Her mother rolled her eyes. 'You've only been back five minutes,' she grumbled, but she rummaged in her purse and handed Jenna the money.

Five minutes later, Jenna rooted through the bin bags until she found her favourite dress – a vintage sundress with a full skirt covered in red cherries. She pulled out her make-up bag and drew a sweep of black liner over her eyelids, added mascara, then finished with a slick of bright red lipstick. She brushed her hair out, backcombed it and tied it back up in a high ponytail. Then she walked out into the street, made her way down to the main road and jumped on the bus. Twenty minutes later she was in Everdene.

By the time she got to the Ship Aground it was jam-packed. Tourists and locals mingled, the tourists pink from the sun. The bar staff poured pint after pint and filled up jugs of sangria. The competition was in full swing. The in-house band provided the music from a list of favourites as contestant after contestant got up to sing.

Jenna signed herself up for the competition before she could change her mind. She read the list of songs to choose from and made her choice. She sat in a corner of the bar and listened. The range of talent was quite varied. Some murdered their songs with good humour, while others took their attempts very seriously.

She was as good as any of them. She knew she was. And suddenly it was her turn. As she stood at the microphone, she remembered all the people who had listened to her sing over the summer, their smiles and their encouragement. She could do it, she knew she could.

She heard the opening bars and her mouth went dry. She grabbed her water and took a quick drink. Then she started to sing. Her voice wavered at first, and no one took any notice of her, thinking she was just another wannabe singer who couldn't hit a note. As her confidence grew, and her voice became stronger, they started to take notice. By the time she had reached the first chorus, people in the crowd were exchanging glances of surprise. She could tell they thought she was good. She smiled and shut her eyes, and her voice soared above the crowd as she took the emotion in the lyrics to another level.

Suddenly she felt as if she was on another plane. The crowd swayed and sang with her, raising their fists in the air to show their appreciation. It was the best feeling in the world.

As the closing bars approached, and she gave the final lyrics her all, she looked across the audience and saw Craig standing at the back. His hands were in his pockets as he watched her. She couldn't read the expression on his face. Her eyes locked with his, and she felt her heart begin to race. Was he going to march up on stage and arrest her? It was what she deserved, after all, but she threw back her shoulders and finished the song, holding the last note for as long as she could.

She finished and there was silence. She met those cool grey eyes defiantly. If he was going to arrest her, she would walk out with dignity. As she stood there waiting, the audience broke into wild applause. There were whistles and whoops and cheers, ten times more than there had been for the people on before her.

In that moment, he smiled, and as she smiled back he gave an approving nod. She came off the stage and pushed through the crowd to-wards him. People patted her on the back as she walked past, saying, 'Well done.' It was a wonderful feeling.

'I need to get out of here,' she told him. 'I need some fresh air.'

She pushed outside into the cool night air, and he followed her. She stood on the patio outside, the sea breeze ruffling her hair.

'That was amazing,' he told her, and she shrugged.

'Yeah, but what am I?' she asked. 'A singer? Or a thief?'

She turned to face him. He smiled at her.

'You're whatever you want to be.'

'You're not going to arrest me?'

'I should.' He looked out towards the shore. The sound of the surf pounding the sand came back at them. 'But I decided something today. I'm going to hand in my notice. I'm not sure I know the difference between right and wrong any more.'

She frowned. 'What I did was wrong. Surely you know that?'

'Yes. But there's a part of me that knows why you did it.' He looked into her eyes. 'And a part of me that knows you won't do it again.'

Someone opened the door and whistled over to her.

'Oi,' they said. 'Come back inside. You've won!'

Jenna looked at Craig. She couldn't believe it. Her heart was pounding as he put his arms round her and pulled her to him, holding her tight.

Jenna went back in and collected her prize money. One hundred pounds, all hers and fairly won. Then she had to go back on stage and sing the song all over again. This time she felt confident, and she looked right over the audience and held Craig's eyes all the way through. He'd believed in her, she thought, and a warm glow filled her heart.

Afterwards, they went outside and sat on the wall to drink the bottle of wine the Ship Aground had given her as part of her prize.

'I handed in the money you stole to the

beach office,' he told her. 'I said I'd found it chucked behind my hut. They said if no one came to claim any of it, they would donate it to charity – the RNLI. They pay for the lifeguards and lifeboats, so it seemed to make sense.'

Jenna nodded her approval. The two of them were silent for a moment. Then Craig put down his glass and took her hand.

'Come on,' he said. 'Let's get out of here.'

They walked back over the sand together and sat on the steps of the beach hut, their bare toes in the sand.

'This started out as the worst day of my life,' said Jenna. 'But it's ended up as the best.'

Craig said nothing, just slid an arm around her shoulder. In front of them, a silver moon hovered in the deep blue sky and a million stars came out to join it.

'You're going to be a star,' he told her.

in the Quick Reads series

Lose yourself
in a good
book with Galaxy®

Curled up on the sofa,
Sunday morning in pyjamas,
just before bed,
in the bath or
on the way to work?

Wherever, whenever,
you can escape
with a good book!

So go on...
indulge yourself with
a good read and the
smooth taste of
Galaxy® chocolate.

Start a new chapter

Quick Reads are brilliant short new books by bestselling authors and celebrities. We hope you enjoyed this one!

Find out more at **www.quickreads.org.uk**

🐦 @Quick_Reads　📘 Quick-Reads

We would like to thank all our funders:

LOTTERY FUNDED

We would also like to thank all our partners in the Quick Reads project for their help and support: NIACE, unionlearn, National Book Tokens, The Reading Agency, National Literacy Trust, Welsh Books Council, The Big Plus Scotland, DELNI, NALA

At Quick Reads, World Book Day and World Book Night we want to encourage everyone in the UK and Ireland to read more and discover the joy of books.

Other Resources

Enjoy this book?

Find out about all the others at **www.quickreads.org.uk**

For Quick Reads audio clips as well as videos
and ideas to help you enjoy reading visit
www.bbc.co.uk/skillswise

Join the Reading Agency's Six Book Challenge at
www.readingagency.org.uk/sixbookchallenge

THE
READING
AGENCY

Find more books for new readers at
www.newisland.ie
www.barringtonstoke.co.uk

Barrington Stoke
cracking reading

Free courses to develop your skills are available in your
local area. To find out more phone 0800 100 900.

National
Careers
Service
Helping you take
the next step